BEANSTALK

E. NESBIT

illustrated by MATT TAVARES

CANDLEWICK PRESS

Jack lived with his mother in a little cottage. It had dormer windows and green shutters whose hinges were so rusty that the shutters wouldn't shut. Jack had taken some of them to make a raft with.

He was always trying to make things that seemed like the things in books—rafts or sledges, or wooden spear-heads to play at savages with, or paper crowns with which to play at kings. He never did any work; and this was very hard on his mother, who took in washing, and had great trouble to make both ends meet. But he did not run away to sea, or set out to seek his fortune, because he knew that that would have broken his mother's heart, and he was very fond of her. Though he wouldn't work, he did useless pretty things for her—brought her bunches of wild-flowers, and made up songs, sad and merry, and sang them to her of an evening. But most of the time he spent in looking at the sky and the clouds and the leaves and the running water, and thinking how beautiful the world was, and how he would love to see every single thing in it. And he always seemed to be trying to dream one particular dream, and never could quite dream it. Sometimes the thought of his mother working so hard while he did nothing would come suddenly upon him, and he would rush off and try to help her, but whatever he did turned out wrong. If he went to draw water he was sure to lose the bucket in the well; if he lifted the wash-tub it always slipped out of his fingers, and then there was the floor to clean as well as the linen to wash all over again. So that it always ended in his mother saying, "Oh, run along, for goodness' sake, and let me get on with my work." And then Jack would go and lie on his front and look at the ants busy among the grass stalks, and make up a pretty poem about the Dignity of Labor, or about how dear and good mothers were.

But poetry, however pretty, is difficult to sell, and the two got poorer and poorer. And at last one day Jack's mother came out to where he was lying on his back watching the clouds go sailing by, and told him that the worst had come.

"No help for it," she said; "we must sell the cow."

"Oh, let me take it to market," cried Jack, jumping up. "I shall pretend to myself I'm a rich farmer with a cow to sell every market-day."

So the rope halter, with Jack at one end of it and the cow at the other, started off down the road.

"Ask five gold pieces for her," said the Mother, "and take what you can get; and don't let the grass grow under your feet."

Jack went along very slowly, and kept his eyes fixed on the ground, because if the grass *did* grow under his feet he wanted to watch it growing.

So this was how it was that he ran plump into something hard, and, looking up, saw a butcher in his wagon.

"Why don't you look where you're going?" the butcher asked crossly.

"Because I thought I might see you," said Jack.

"Ha! I see you're a clever boy," said the butcher, not at all offended. "Thinking of selling your cow?"

"Well," said Jack, "that was rather the idea."

"And what's the price?"

"Five gold pieces," said Jack boldly.

"I wouldn't rob you of her by offering such a poor price," said the butcher kindly. "Look here."

He pulled out a handful of large, bright-colored beans.

"Aren't they beautiful?" he said.

"Oh, they are—they are!" said Jack. And they were. They had all the colors and all the splendor of precious stones.

"Well, is it a bargain?" the butcher asked.

"Oh, yes," said Jack. "Take the ugly old cow."

And with that he took the beans, thrust the end of the rope into the butcher's hand, and hurried off toward home.

I don't think I had better tell you what happened when he told his mother what he had done. You can perhaps guess. I will only say that it ended in his mother throwing the beans out of the window and sending Jack to bed without his supper. Then she spent the evening ironing, and every now and then a tear fell down and hissed and fizzled on the hot iron.

The next morning Jack woke up feeling very hot and half choked. He found his room rather darker than usual, and at first he decided that it was too early to get up; then as he was just snuggling the blanket closer round his neck he saw what it was that was shutting out the sunshine. The beans had grown up into a huge twisted stalk with immense leaves. When Jack ran to the window and pushed his hand out among the green he could see no top to the plant. It seemed to grow right up into the sky.

Then suddenly Jack was a changed boy. Something wonderful had happened to him, and it had made him different. It sometimes happens to people that they see or hear something quite wonderful, and then they are never altogether the same again.

Jack scrambled into his clothes, ran to the door, and shouted: "Mother, those beautiful beans have grown! I told you I'd made a good bargain with that silly old cow. I'm going to climb up and see what's at the top."

And before his mother could stop him he was out of the window and up the beanstalk, climbing and wriggling among the branches, and when she reached the window he was almost out of sight. She stood looking up after him till she couldn't see him any more, and then she sighed, and went to her son's untidy room, to make his bed and set all straight for him.

Jack climbed on and on until his head felt dizzy and his legs and arms ached. He had had no supper last night, you remember, and no breakfast before he started. But at last there was no more stalk to climb, and as soon as he reached the top tendril it suddenly flattened and opened out before him into a long white dusty road.

He was in a new land, and as far as he could see nothing else was alive in that land but himself. The trees were withered, the fields were bare, and every stream had run dry. Altogether it was not at all a nice place; but if it wasn't nice it was new; and besides, he could not face the idea of going down that beanstalk again without anything to eat, and he set out to look for a house and beg a breakfast.

At that moment something dark
came between him and the light—
fluttered above his head, and then settled
on the road beside him.

"Oh, mercy! I though it was a great bird," cried
Jack. But it wasn't. It was a fairy—Jack knew that
at once, though he had never seen one before.
There are some things you cannot mistake.

"Well, Jack," said the fairy, "I've been looking
for you."

"I believe I've been looking for you all my life,
if you come to that," said Jack.

"Yes, you have," said the fairy. "Now listen."

She told Jack a story that made him all hot, and cold, and ashamed, and eager to do something heroic at once, for she explained how the new land he had found had once belonged to his father, who was a good and great man, and who had ruled his land well and been loved by his subjects. But unfortunately one of his subjects happened to be a giant, and, being naturally of a large size, he considered himself more important than anyone else, and he had killed Jack's father, and with the help of a bad fairy had imprisoned the faithful subjects in the trees.

Since the giant's rule began the land had not flourished—nothing would grow on it, the houses fell down in ruins and the waters ran dry. So the giant had shut himself and his wife up in a large white house with his precious belongings, and there he lived his selfish, horrid life.

"Now," said the fairy, "the time has come for you to set things straight. And this is really what you've been trying to dream about all your life. You must find the giant and get back your father's land for your mother. She has worked for you all your life. Now you will work for her; but you have the best of it, because her work was mending and washing and cooking and scrubbing, and your work is—adventures. Go straight on and do the things that first come into your head. This is good advice in ordinary life, and it works well in this land too. Goodbye."

And with a flutter of sea-green, shining wings the fairy vanished, and Jack was left staring into nothingness. He didn't stare long though, for, as I said before, he was a changed boy. There are plenty of people who could go in for adventures splendidly, but somehow they are never able to do anything else, and if they don't happen to fall in with adventures they can do nothing but dream of them, and so have a poor time of it in this world. Jack was one of these people. Only he, you see, had got out of this world and had fallen in with adventures into the bargain.

He went along the road, and when he came to a large white house the first thing he thought of doing was, curiously enough, to knock at the door and ask for something to eat, just as you or I would have done if we had gone up a large beanstalk without our breakfast or our last night's supper.

"Go away!" said the little old woman who opened the door, just as many people do if you ask them for something to eat and they don't happen to know you. "My husband is a giant, and he'll eat you if he sees you."

"You needn't let him see me," said Jack. "I haven't had anything to eat for *ages*. Do give me something, there's a good sort!"

So she took him in and gave him some bread and butter and a poached egg, and before he was half-way through it the whole house began to shake, and the old woman seized Jack, put his eggy plate into his hand, and pushed him into the oven and closed the door.

Jack had the sense not to call out, and he finished his egg in the oven. Then he found he could see through the crack near the hinges, so he glued his eye to it and saw!

He saw the giant—a great big fat man with red hair and mutton-chop whiskers. The giant flung himself down at the table and roared for his dinner, and his trembling old wife brought him a whole hog, which he tore in pieces in his hands and ate without any manners, and he didn't offer his wife so much as a piece of the crackling. When he had finished he licked his great greasy fingers and called out:

"Bring me my hen!"

Jack was rather surprised. He thought it was a curious creature to have on the dinner-table. But the next instant he understood, for the hen stood on the table, and every time the giant said *"Lay!"* it laid a golden egg.

It went on doing this until Jack thought it must be really tired, and until the giant *was,* for he lay back in his chair and fell asleep.

The first thing that occurred to Jack to do was to leap out of the oven, seize the hen under his arm, and make off for the beanstalk and his home as fast as ever he could.

I won't describe the scene in the cottage when he arrived. His mother was inclined to scold him, but when she thoroughly understood about the hen she kissed him instead, and said that she had always believed he would do something clever, some day. Jack sold golden eggs at the market every week, and his mother gave up taking in washing; but she still went on cleaning the cottage herself. I believe she rather liked that kind of work.

Then suddenly one morning, as Jack stood in the cottage garden with his hands in the pockets of a quite new pair of breeches, he felt he couldn't go on living without another journey up the beanstalk, and forgetting to tell his mother that he might not be in to dinner, he was off and up. He found the same dry, withered land at the top, and, although he was not hungry this time, he couldn't think of anything new to say, so he said the same thing to the old woman; but this time he found it much harder to get round her, although she did not know him again. Either his face was changed, or the breeches were a complete disguise.

"No," she kept on saying, and Jack lost his temper when she had said it twenty-two times.

"A boy came here before, and he was a bad one and a thief, and I can't let another boy in."

"But I've got an honest face," said Jack. "Everybody says so."

"That's true," said the woman, and she let him in.

This time he was obliged to hide before he had begun to eat, and he was rather glad, because, as I said, he was not hungry—the giant's wife had only given him bread and cheese, and the cheese was rather stale. When they heard the giant coming along the road the woman lifted the copper lid and made Jack get in.

The giant seemed in a good temper, for he chucked his wife under the chin and said: *"Fresh meat today, my dear. I can smell it."*

"I'm—I'm afraid you're wrong," said his wife; and Jack could hear by the way she said it that she was very frightened. "It's half the ox you had yesterday, and that fresh meat you smell is just a bit of a dead cart-horse that a crow dropped on the roof."

The giant seemed sulky after that, and didn't eat his dinner with much appetite, and when his wife was clearing away he suddenly laid hold of her and shouted: *"Bring me my money-bags!"*

Jack couldn't help lifting up the copper lid a little bit when he heard the chink of the coins, and when he saw the giant counting out the great heap of gold he longed to have it for his own, for he knew that it ought by rights to belong to him or his mother.

Presently the giant fell asleep, and Jack looked all round to see if the wife was about before he dared to get out of the copper. And he heard her walking about upstairs, so he jumped out, seized on the bags, and again made off for the beanstalk.

He reached home as his mother was clearing away the dinner-plates; but I won't describe the scene. Of course they were now rich, and Jack wished to live in a large house, but his mother said she couldn't leave the "bits of things," and when he came to think it over Jack felt that he couldn't bear to leave the beanstalk.

Another day came when Jack felt he must make another journey to the giant's land, disguised in a new smock-frock and gaiters, and again the same thing happened, except that it was harder than ever to persuade the giant's wife to take him in. She did at last, however, after explaining that two boys had served her badly, and that if he turned out bad too, then the giant would most likely kill her. No sooner was Jack inside the house than the giant was heard coming. The woman showed Jack an empty barrel, and he crept under it.

Then the giant came in, and he rolled his eyes, twisted his great head about, and swore that he smelt fresh meat. His wife told him he was wrong, but this time he didn't believe her, and he looked in the copper and in the oven and in the bread-crock, and under the sink; but he never thought of the empty barrel—partly, I daresay, because he thought it was full of something that it wasn't full of.

At last he gave up the search and sat down to his dinner, and when he had finished he stretched himself until Jack thought some of his buttons would burst, and called:

"Wife, bring me my harp!"

The old woman brought in a beautiful golden harp, which she set on the table, and as soon as the giant said, *"Play!"* it began to give out beautiful soothing music, and the giant presently fell asleep, while his wife went into the back kitchen to wash up.

The first thing that occurred to Jack was to upset the barrel, dash to the table, and take the harp, but as his hands touched it it cried out in a human voice, "Master, master!" For one second Jack nearly dropped it; then he realized that the giant was waking. He rushed to the door, kicking the cat in his hurry as he heard the giant stumble out after him.

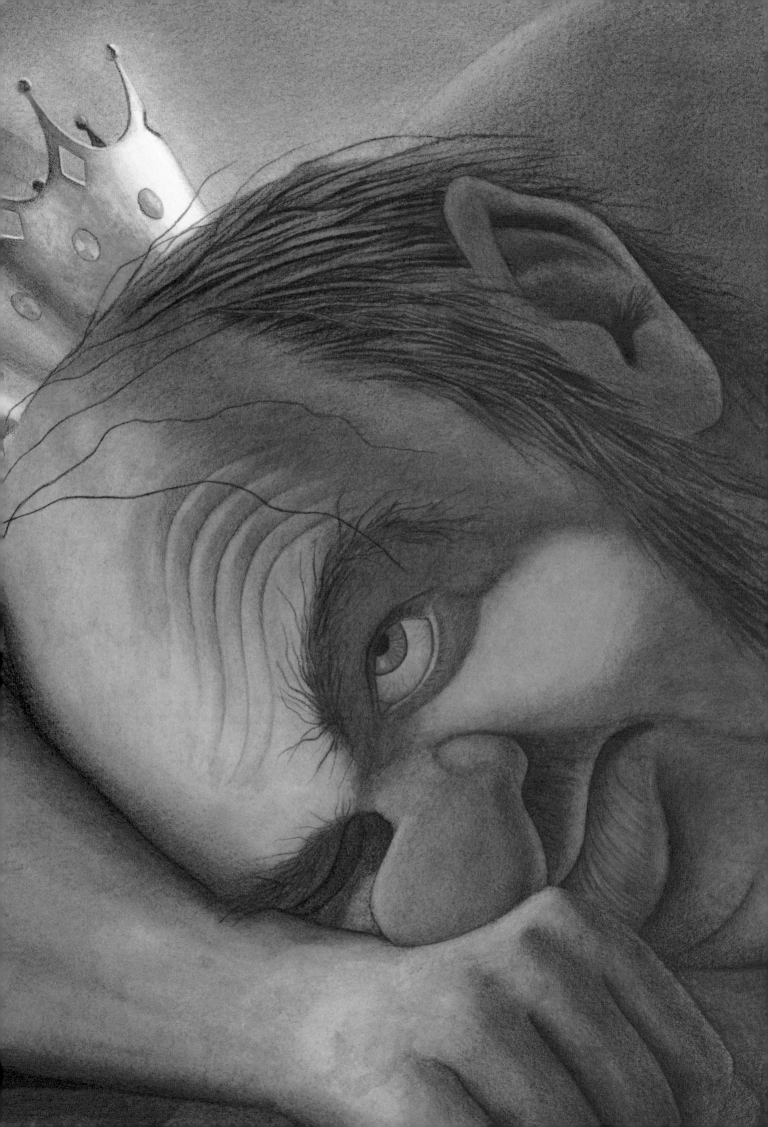

But the giant was heavy and only half awake, and by the time Jack was down the beanstalk the giant was only just at the top; but he was coming down, that was quite plain, for the next moment the great beanstalk shook and shivered with his great weight. Jack screamed to his mother for a chopper, and, like the good woman she was, she brought it without asking what it was for.

Jack hacked at the beanstalk, and it cut like butter, so that when it fell the giant fell down with it and was killed, and that was the end of him.

And now Jack and his mother had plenty to live upon, and might have rented a palace if they had liked, but still Jack's mother wouldn't leave her cottage.

As for the enchanted land up above — well, the fairy told Jack that after the death of the giant the people came out of the trees, and the land flourished under the rule of the giant's wife, a most worthy woman, whose only fault was that she was too ready to trust boys.

The End

To my mother, Jane Tavares
M. T.

Special thanks to Kara LaReau, Caroline Lawrence, Chris Paul,
Rosemary Stimola, Christopher Bing, Timothy Sawyer, Lee Petrie,
Sarah Tavares, Ava Tavares, and all my friends and family
who helped with this project. —M. T.

First edition 2006
Text originally published in *The Old Nursery Stories* in 1908

Library of Congress Cataloging-in-Publication Data

Nesbit, E. (Edith), 1858–1924
Jack and the beanstalk / E. Nestbit ; illustrated by Matt Tavares.—1st ed.
p. cm.
Summary: After climbing to the top of a huge
beanstalk, a boy uses his quick wits to outsmart a giant
and gain a fortune for himself and his mother.
ISBN 978-0-7636-2124-7
[1. Fairy tales. 2. Giants—Folklore. 3. Folklore—England.]
I. Tavares, Matt, ill. II. Jack and the beanstalk. English. III. Title.
PZ8.N365Jac 2006
398.2—dc22
[E]   2005050190

09 10 11 12 13 14 CCP 10 9 8 7 6 5

Printed in Shenzhen, Guangdong, China

This book was typeset in Garamond.
The illustrations were done in pencil and watercolor.

Candlewick Press
99 Dover Street
Somerville, Massachusetts 02144

visit us at www.candlewick.com